WANDA AND HER FURRY FRIENDS

By Geraldine D. Villalba

BookBaby

Pennsauken, NJ

Print ISBN: 978-1-09830-677-9

Printed in the United States of America on SFI Certified paper.

First Edition

Cover Art by Timothy Hutto
Illustrations by Ed Hutto

ACKNOWLEDGEMENTS

With special thanks to Tim Hutto, who took time away from his family and busy schedule building log cabins in Idaho to interpret my ideas and create the beautiful cover for my book.

And also to Eddie Hutto, the multi-talented artist and craftsman who drew all the illustrations that bring my book to life. He lives in a log cabin with his family in the Idaho mountains and his excellent work indeed deserves recognition.

To

Abbie, the youngest of my 9 grandchildren

And to Heath and Ian, my new great grandchildren.

May your imaginations grow and thrive.

TAIL NUMBER ONE

Wanda sat and rocked and rocked in her grandmother's old rocking chair that was out on the front porch of their house. She was thinking about how she could help her mom and dad make some money to help pay the mortgage. It was too late in the year to think about a lemonade stand. Last year she made $25 selling lemonade, which was wonderful, but now the bank note was due next week. As she walked back and forth, she looked over to the side and saw something glinting in the sun. Her curiosity got the better of her, so she got up and went over to see what it was. She rubbed the dirt away with her foot and lo and behold it was a beautiful silver dollar. "Oh my!" she said and she began to look around to see if she could find any more. After a few minutes, she found five more beautiful silver dollars. "I had better look to find something to put this into," she said. She spied an old basket leaning on its side beneath a big old tree. She picked up the basket and put the silver dollars inside. As she did this, she noticed that someone had placed branches neatly, one behind the other as if trying to hide something. She took the branches away and found a very large opening in the tree trunk. She walked over to it and peered inside. It was very dark. "I need to go home and get some light," she said. She ran home, went into the kitchen, looked in the drawer and found a trusty flashlight which she slipped into her back pocket. Then she looked around for her old camping lantern which had a very bright light. At last she could now investigate the tunnel. She ran over to the opening but hesitated. It was rather dark inside and she was a little bit afraid. "I sure hope there aren't any large spiders in there," she said to herself. "I really don't like spiders. They have way too many legs."

Feeling a little braver she began to walk through the tunnel and came to a door. "Now what is a door doing here?" she asked herself. Timidly she knocked on the door and heard a sweet voice call out and say "Come in, Wanda."

"My goodness who knows my name down here?" she asked. She opened the door and stepped inside. Sitting in front of her was the the cutest looking little hedgehog. "Hello Wanda," she said. "My name is Aerial. When I was born, my master told me that I had a very important job to do. Please walk over to the cabinet, open the door and take what is inside, because it belongs to you." Wanda walked over to the cabinet, opened the door and found a green velvet bag sitting on the shelf. She picked it up and it jingled. After peering inside, she found more silver dollars.

"Take it and put the cord over your wrist," Aerial instructed her. "But we must hurry and leave as we have lots of other things to do!" She hurried Wanda out of the room and down the corridor they went.

Soon they found another door. Aerial knocked, opened it and went inside, where they found a sophisticated-looking red fox doing her nails. She looked up and said

"Please come in. My name is Bettina." Then she giggled. Bettina was always giggling. "Wanda, I have a very important job to do, so please go over to the cabinet, look inside and take what you see because it belongs to you."

Wanda went over to the cabinet and found another green velvet bag into which she peered and saw more silver dollars. "We must hurry as it is getting very late," Bettina said.

"Late for what?" Wanda wondered.

They left Bettina's room and walked down the corridor. They came to another door upon which Bettina knocked. "Come in," a sleepy voice called out. Upon entering the room, Wanda saw a big, grey angora cat stretched out on an old settee. He had a big orange bow around his neck and the fluffiest tail Wanda had ever seen. When Wanda commented on this, Aerial just shrugged her shoulders and said "Yes, he dusts all the furniture around here. He keeps things neat and tidy."

"Hello Wanda," the kitty said. "You are finally here. My name is Casper and I have a very important job to do. Go into that cabinet over there and take what rightfully belongs to you." When Wanda opened the cabinet, she found still another green velvet bag with silver dollars, and she slipped the cord over her wrist.

"We must hurry as it is getting very late," urged Casper. So, they hurriedly left Casper's room and went down the corridor until they came upon an impressive looking door that had purple iris painted all down the front of it. Casper knocked on it and a big, booming voice called out "Come in! Come in children." They all walked into the room and there sitting on a high stool in front of a round table was a funny little man with a large hump on his back. "Come in, come in children."

By his left side was a large coal-black Doberman named Ebony and on his right side was a big fat rabbit called Mr. Dillon.

"My name is Mr. Hump-frees", he introduced himself. "Well, Wanda my dear, I am so glad you are finally here. As you probably know by now, we all have a very important job to do, and so let us get on with it because the time is passing quickly. Open that cabinet over there and take out what you find." Wanda did as she was told and found a large red velvet bag which she opened and discovered many more silver dollars.

"This is really heavy," she said as she picked it up.

"Pour all of your silver dollars out on the table, as we must count them," instructed Mr. Hump-frees. Carefully, Wanda poured all of her dollars out on the table and began to count them. When she was finished counting the money, Mr. Hump-frees smiled and said, "Does that amount ring any bells in your memory?"

"My goodness! The amount is exactly what we owe the bank," Wanda said. 'That is so curious!" Then everyone smiled.

"But it is so late," Mr. Hump-frees exclaimed as he pushed the money into an old milk pail and handed the pail to Wanda. "You must leave now, my dear, or else you will have to remain here with us forever." A startled Wanda began to move toward the door. She was sad as she did not want to leave her new-found friends, but she did not want to remain down here forever either. She blew them all kisses and ran down the corridor. She was just able to squeeze through the door and outside.

"Whew, that was close" she said aloud. As she looked again toward the opening in the tree trunk, it completely disappeared. She then ran home with both arms hugging the old milk pail close to her body.

Her mom opened the door and an excited Wanda began to relate her adventure and handed the milk pail to her mother. "What is this?" her mom asked. Excitedly, Wanda continued her story.

"My word, your imagination is working overtime," her mom said. "I think you fell asleep and dreamed all of this. These silver dollars must have been buried by your Grandfather a long time ago."

The next day, Wanda traveled into town with her folks to the local bank. They were greeted warmly by the manager, Mr. Wilson. Wanda's dad placed the bag of silver dollars on his desk.

"What have we here?" Mr. Wilson asked with great surprise. "I have not seen this many silver dollars in years! "

"We think our daughter Wanda here dug these out of a cache that had to have been buried there by my eccentric Father-in-Law a good many years ago."

"Please allow my loan officer to take a look at these and determine if they might be part of a robbery that happened back in the '30s," Mr. Wilson said.

The loan officer examined the collection and was able to determine that they were indeed not connected with that robbery. "Your coins are dated mostly from the 1940's and what we are looking for are dated from the 30's," he said. "So, these are definitely not from that robbery."

Mr. Wilson smiled and said, "Well, then, I guess it is safe to stamp your documents 'Paid in Full'". Then Mr. Wilson put out his hand and shook with Wanda's father. "It was nice to do business with you."

"And we intend to continue to do business with you. Good bye, Mr. Wilson."

As they left the bank building, Wanda's mom explained that she wanted to stop at the market to pick up "some things".

"Such an event as this deserves celebrating, don't you think?"

And they did indeed celebrate.

TAIL NUMBER TWO

The summer had been long and hot, and Wanda was feeling boredom setting in, especially after her exciting adventure finding all those silver dollars. She went into the kitchen and made herself a sandwich and put it into a plastic bag. Then she plopped it into her backpack. She called out to her mom saying she was going to walk over to the old wishing well that her grandfather made for her grandmother so many years ago.

"I won't be gone long," she said.

"Okay, honey," her mother called back.

Wanda walked out the front door and down the path to the well.

She was preparing to sit down on the side of the well when her gaze spotted Aerial at the bottom. "Aerial, what are you doing down there?"

"Hurry down here Wanda if you do not want to be late for tea." When Wanda heard the invitation, she climbed over the side and down into the well. As this was not a real well, it was not deep. She followed the little hedgehog through a large opening into the most beautiful place Wanda had ever seen. Before her eyes were acres and acres of yellow daisies, as far as she could see. Hopping around in the daisies was Mr. Dillon, the big fat bunny.

And barking furiously at the big fat bunny's antics was Ebony. Such a chaotic and noisy scene caused Wanda to put her hands over her ears. But she kept an eye on Aerial and watched her make a turn in the road. Wanda ran after her, and when she made the turn in the road, she saw the most charming little cottage with smoke coming from a red chimney. Aerial knocked on the door, opened it, then motioned to Wanda to follow her inside.

Upon entering the cottage Wanda saw Mr. Hump-frees sitting in a big comfortable chair in front of a brick fireplace smoking a pipe. Laying stretched out full length was Casper the grey Persian cat. Wanda could hear dishes rattling in the kitchen and out came Bettina carrying a tray with mugs of hot tea.

"Take the green mug, Wanda. I knew you were coming." And she giggled. Bettina was always giggling.

Wanda found a comfortable chair to sit in and began a conversation with Mr. Hump-frees. She told him what her family did with the silver dollars.

"Ah, that is just fine," he said. Then Mr. Hump-frees told Wanda about his childhood which was very interesting and led to the story of how he came to add the little menagerie to his own life. "I found Aerial stuck in a mud hole. The poor little thing was exhausted from trying to dig herself out of it. She was very grateful that I had freed her and she has been with me ever since.

"I caught Bettina by surprise with eggs she had stolen from my hen house, one in each paw. When I asked her what she was doing, she told me that she was very hungry, so I let her have the eggs. She was grateful and she has been with me ever since. Actually, she is pretty handy in the kitchen.

"I found Casper under my stairs one rainy night and he was wet and hungry. I brought him inside and fed him, and he has been with me ever since. Ebony and Mr. Dillon came as a pair. They have been close friends for a long time. But now Ebony is one of my closest friends, too." Just then they all heard a thumping sound, and it was Mr. Dillon coming inside, very excited.

"Wanda, Wanda," he cried. "Someone in the real world is looking for you. I heard them call, Wanda, where are you?"

"Oh, my goodness. That is my Mom. I told her I would only be gone for a short time and here it is five o'clock!" Wanda then jumped out of the comfortable chair in which she was sitting. "I must leave now," and she blew them all a kiss and ran out the door.

Wanda's mom was shocked to find her daughter climbing out of the wishing well. "Wanda, what are you doing in the wishing well?" she asked. She helped Wanda as she climbed over the side of the well.

"I am happy that school is starting again soon," Wanda's mother sighed. "But it is late and it is already getting very dark. I think we will have to run the rest of the way home."

And they both ran down the path to the welcoming lights of their home.

TAIL NUMBER THREE

Wanda awakened feeling very energetic. "I think I will make a blackberry cobbler for dessert tonight," she said. "And I know where I can find the biggest, most luscious berries ever."

She went into the kitchen, opened a cabinet and found a colander into which she would put the berries. She needed to go to the south pasture. Her parents did not like her to go there so she did not go very often. As this was where the berries grew, she thought she would not be there long.

Sure enough there were the most beautiful berries hanging from the vines. She began to pick them, stopping just long enough to plop a big juicy one into her mouth. While she picked the fruit, she noticed a lean-to snuggled in the midst of a grove of cedar trees. Curious that she never noticed it before, she wandered over and looked inside. Sitting on a table was her beloved doll house--the one her dad made for her when she was 5 years old and that she loved and played with every day for years. The memory brought a tear to her eyes. Lovingly she removed the roof and looked inside. Then a funny thing happened. She was inside the doll house jubilantly running from room to room and sitting on chairs and the bed and on the sofa. As she sat on the sofa wondering how it happened that she was inside the doll house, an excited Aerial came running down the hallway. "Oh Wanda, I am so happy to see you! We need your help. Casper was dusting with his glorious tail and it got snapped into a mouse trap. The mouse trap is nailed to the floor and Casper is stuck there. We need you to open the trap."

"Show me where he is," Wanda said.

She released the trap and Casper gave her one of his rare "Cheshire Cat" grins and then scampered off. Aerial thanked Wanda and scampered off also. Wanda then picked up the colander of berries and walked out the door. Magically, she had returned to her normal size. As she started for home, she had this eerie feeling, turned around and found that she was being tracked by a mountain lion.

She panicked and tried to think of what she could do. But then suddenly Mr. Hump-frees and all of Wanda's furry friends appeared, circling the big cat who now looked confused.

"Don't worry Wanda," said Mr. Hump-frees. "I have a plan."

He then put his right hand inside of his jacket and pulled out a slingshot. With his left hand he reached into his pocket and brought out a large shiny stone. Ker-plunk! Right in the middle of the mountain lion's forehead it hit. The surprised lion jumped three feet into the air and ran off in the opposite direction.

"Run home as fast as you can, keeping your eye out for the mountain lion," Mr. Hump-frees instructed.

"Oh, thank you all my friends," Wanda cried. And she ran home as fast as she could. When she got home, she decided not to say anything about her experience to her Mom as she did not want to frighten her. She made her way about the kitchen preparing to make the cobbler. She was still shaking from her close call, but she was determined to put the entire episode out of her thoughts. After dinner later that night and after her parents exclaimed that the cobbler was the best they had ever eaten, Wanda's dad said that he had talked with their neighbor Mr. McGinty. He had told him that several neighbors saw a mountain lion prowling around and that he should get out his rifle, load it, and keep it handy.

Pretty good advice, I think.

TAIL NUMBER FOUR

School had started. Wanda had always dreamed of being a veterinarian. She had applied at a college that was located 50 miles north of the area where she lived and had been accepted. She was looking forward to college and could hardly wait until she finished high school.

When she graduated from college a full-fledged veterinarian, she received a small check from her parents with which she would begin her business. She looked hard for a suitable place to start and she finally found an empty little cottage that was just perfect, but very dirty and needed paint badly. With the help of her parents and friends, this huge task was done. And now she could open for business.

On her first day, a tall man who was bald with wiry wisps of hair above both ears, rushed into her clinic. He placed a bundle into her arms saying earnestly, "If you can fix my Trixie good as new, I will print a full-page ad of your clinic in my newspaper." He was the editor of The Daily Bee. Wanda liked the sound of a full-page ad and she took the little dog into the examining room. She found that Trixie had a broken left hind leg and a couple of minor wounds. Wanda set the leg and washed and tended the wounds. She gave the dog back to her owner with instructions on how to care for Trixie.

A few days later, Wanda opened the newspaper and there, true to his word, the editor had placed her ad.

She ripped the page from the paper and neatly folded it and put it in her desk drawer. She loved it, and she would take it out and look at it many times each day.

Wanda's clinic did very well and it wasn't too long before she knew that she needed help. She put an ad in the Daily Bee. Soon she was interviewing applicants but she had her eye on one tall, very handsome man named Mark Wilson. Wilson? Could he be the son of the bank manager, she wondered? Wanda was glad she chose Mark because they fell in love and were soon married. They had two children---Lorrie and Bobby. As the children grew older, Bobby was always getting into mischief and giving his sister a hard time as she tried to look after him

TAIL NUMBER FIVE

One day Lorrie, now seven years old, was in the kitchen of their home taking the dishes out of the dishwasher and putting them away, when she looked out the window and watched four-year-old Bobby running after two squirrels who were chasing each other. The squirrels ran into the forest which was near their home. Bobby ran after them and into the forest. Both children had been instructed not to play in the forest unless they were with an adult.

"Oh darn. I guess I need to go get Bobby. He knows he should not go into the forest," Lorrie thought.

Lorrie ran out the door after Bobby. When she reached the entrance to the forest she hesitated. Timidly she looked into the dark trees and called to her little brother. But no answer. Walking slowly into the forest, she hoped she would see him right away, but no such luck. Going further inside was necessary, and she kept on calling his name. But no answer.

At last she found him sitting on a fallen log, crying very hard. Bobby stopped crying when he saw his sister and ran into her arms saying, "I am losted."

"No, you are not," Lorrie told him firmly. But of course, they were now both "losted". She grabbed Bobby's hand and pulled him along a makeshift path until they came to a large clearing. Sitting in the middle of the clearing was an honest to goodness Indian-type teepee. Lorrie cautioned Bobby to not say a word so they could sneak up to the tent and see who lived there. As they got closer, a funny little man opened the flap of the tent and greeted them.

"Hello Lorrie and Bobby," he said. "We have been waiting for you to arrive. Come in, come in," he invited them. Lorrie wondered how he knew their names.

"You are Wanda's children, aren't you?" he asked. Well, if he knew their mother then he must be all right, Lorrie thought. They entered the teepee and it was quite large inside, much larger than it looked from the outside.

"I am Mr. Hump-frees," he said, "And these are my friends." He pointed to a group sitting alongside a kind of fire-pit. "Please meet Aerial and Bettina. And that sleepy fellow laying stretched out is Casper. Then there is Mr. Dillon and my best friend Ebony." When he saw the dog, Bobby let out a whoop and dashed over to him, threw his arms around his neck and planted a big wet kiss on the top of his head.

"Bobby!!" Lorrie cried out. "We are guests here."

"Don't be angry with him, Lorrie, I kind of liked it," said Ebony. Then everyone laughed.

Mr. Hump-frees asked Bettina to fix a snack so they would not be hungry on their journey. Lorrie and Bobby wondered what journey he was talking about. When all had finished eating, Mr. Hump-frees went over to the wall and pushed a button. The entire wall slid open revealing two small, brightly painted cars and lots and lots of track. Mr. Hump-frees helped Lorrie and Bobby into the back seat of the first car and tightened their seat belts. Then he invited his furry friends to get into the second car. After adjusting their belts, he got into the front seat, pressed a lever and they were off!

"Venice, first stop!" he called out.

Soon they were driving by canals and very old buildings, past the railroad station and on to Florence where they saw the statue of David. Then on to Rome where they stopped for a gelato, much to Bobby's satisfaction. Next was Paris and the Eifel Tower. Then on to Germany, Sweden, Finland and Denmark. After visiting Japan, Mr. Hump-frees said that China would be their last stop. As they left China, Mr. Hump-frees told Lorrie and Bobby that he could see their mommy on the front porch looking for them. The little cars stopped and the children got off. They waved good bye to their special friends, blowing kisses, and the cars disappeared down the track. The children saw their mom and ran to her.

"Oh Mom," Lorrie said breathlessly, "You are not going to believe the wonderful adventure we just had." Their mom laughed and said "Oh, yes I will! But tell me all about it over supper." And with that they all went inside.

The next day was the busiest ever at Wanda's clinic, and when the last patient left and the door was closed and locked, Wanda almost ran into her little office and collapsed into her favorite chair.

"What a day" she muttered. She suddenly glanced up and out the window. A little red fox was running down the road. "That cannot be Bettina. Could it?" Suddenly the little fox turned and was smiling and giggling. It was Bettina! Then Wanda heard a chugging noise and a vintage 1940 open car came into view. Mr. Hump-frees was behind the steering wheel. Next to him was his faithful friend Ebony, and in the back were Mr. Dillon, Aerial and Casper. The car drove up to where Bettina stood waiting and she ran around the front of the car and slid into the seat next to Ebony. All the furry friends and Mr. Hump-frees turned and looked at Wanda. They all waved, jumping up and down, smiling all the while. Then the car merrily chugged down the road until it completely disappeared

THE END